How Angel Peterson Got His Name

Also by Gary Paulsen

GARY PAULSEN

How Angel Peterson Got His Name

And other outrageous tales
about extreme sports

WENDY
LAMB
BOOKS

Published by
Wendy Lamb Books
an imprint of
Random House Children's Books
a division of Random House, Inc.
1540 Broadway
New York, New York 10036

Wendy Lamb Books is a trademark of Random House, Inc.

Visit us on the Web! www.randomhouse.com/kids
Educators and librarians, for a variety of teaching tools, visit us at
www.randomhouse.com/teachers

Library of Congress Cataloging-in-Publication Data

Paulsen, Gary.
  How Angel Peterson got his name / Gary Paulsen.
      p. cm.
Summary: Author Gary Paulsen relates tales from his youth in a small town in
northwestern Minnesota in the late 1940s and early 1950s, such as skiing behind
a souped-up car and imitating daredevil Evel Knievel.
  ISBN 0-385-72949-9 (trade) — ISBN 0-385-90090-2 (lib. bdg.) 1. Paulsen,
Gary—Childhood and youth—Juvenile literature. 2. Authors, American—20th
century—Biography—Juvenile literature. [1. Paulsen, Gary—Childhood and
youth. 2. Authors, American.] I. Title.
  PS3566.A834 Z467 2003
  813'.54—dc21

                                                                    2002007668

The text of this book is set in 11.75-point Charter.
Book design by Melissa J Knight

Printed in the United States of America
January 2003
10 9 8 7 6 5 4 3
BVG

 This book is dedicated to all boys in their thirteenth year; the miracle is that we live through it.

Foreword

In order to bring this book into the now, and connect it to my present life, I want to tell you about two incidents.

First, my own wonderful madness: I was twelve, living in a little northern Minnesota town that had a river and a small dam with perhaps a twelve-foot fall of water across the spillway. Remember these facts: waterfall, twelve-foot drop.

I had read an article in a men's magazine called "The Fools Who Shoot the Falls," which described several men who tried to achieve fame by going over Niagara Falls in a barrel.

There was . . . something . . . about it that

drew me. I completely ignored the fact that the idea of falling a hundred or so feet in a barrel was incredibly stupid. If you proposed just to jam a man in a barrel, take him up on a rope and drop him a hundred feet into a duck pond it's probable that there would be very few takers.

But for some reason the waterfall changed everything. Oh, sure, you'd still drop a hundred or so feet, still achieve terminal velocity, still probably die. Almost all the people who have tried Niagara Falls have been killed. But that waterfall . . . that made it worth doing.

Or, as I later told my best friend, Carl Peterson, it seemed like a good idea at the time.

And so I found an old wooden pickle barrel with oak staves, and after carefully reinforcing it by wrapping it with about two hundred feet of clothesline and miles of electrical tape (this was before duct tape) I lined the inside of it with an old quilt, set it on the bank near the top of the spillway, climbed into the barrel, wedged the lid in place over my head and threw myself back and forth inside until the barrel wobbled off the bank.

"Are you all right?" I asked.

He nodded. "Sure . . ."

"Why are you walking so funny?"

"Oh, no reason. I was doing something out by the goat barn and thought I'd try a little experiment. . . ."

"Pee on the electric fence?"

He studied me for a moment, then nodded. "How did you know?"

"It's apparently genetic," I said, turning back to work. "It's something some of us have to do. Like climbing Everest."

"Will I ever stop doing things like this?"

And I wanted to lie to him, tell him that as he grew older he would become wise and sensible, but then I thought of my own life: riding Harley motorcycles and crazy horses, running Iditarods, sailing single-handed on the Pacific.

I shook my head. "It's the way we are."

"Well," he sighed, tugging at his pants to ease the swelling, "at least I know what *that's* like and don't have to pee on any more fences."

And he waddled into his room.

I'm not exactly sure what I expected. I might have had a thought that the barrel was made of wood, which floats. Therefore the whole craft would float, bobbing to the edge of the spillway and then over to drop to the water below, and would lead me to everlasting fame as the first boy to go over the Eighth Street dam in a barrel.

Instead the barrel sank. Like a stone. Straight to the bottom, which was about six feet down, where it bumped around a bit while I panicked. To my horror, I discovered that the lid had swelled enough with the water to be sealed in place, that the barrel was fast filling up with water, that pickle barrels were amazingly strong and you could not kick them apart from the inside, and that I would gain fame only as the first boy stupid enough to drown himself in a barrel.

But because there is a fate that sometimes protects idiots, a swirl of current caught the barrel and lifted it to the edge of the spillway, where it teetered once or twice before it dropped off the edge to fall the twelve feet to the river below. There it would merely have sunk again had not the same fate intervened to cause the barrel to slam down on a sharp rock exactly the way it needed to in order to break into fifteen or twenty small pieces and leave me stunned, with a bleeding nose, sitting on the bank below the dam contemplating the fickleness of fate, which endowed me with an uncanny, lifelong ability to identify with the hapless coyote in the Road Runner cartoons.

The second incident shows that nothing really changes. I had written a book about my life with my cousin Harris and talked about Harris peeing on an electric fence. The shock made him do a backflip and he swore he could see a rainbow in the pee. Many readers, especially women, were amazed that a boy would be insane enough to do this and didn't believe that it had happened. However, I did get many letters from men saying that either they or a brother or cousin or friend had tried the same stunt, with some exciting results. One man said it allowed him to see into the past.

I was sitting writing one day when my son, then thirteen, came into the house with a sheepish look on his deathly pale face. As he passed me, I couldn't help noticing that he was waddling.

A Note of Caution

While extreme sports have advanced incredibly since I was young—people do things with skateboards and snowboards in the X Games that are so hairy it's hard to believe anybody lives through them—I want you to remember two important facts:

1. We were quite a bit dumber then.
2. There wasn't any safety gear.

There were no helmets, for instance, other than old football helmets made of stiff leather or army surplus ones made of steel (some with bullet holes in them), and they were so heavy that they caused more trouble than wearing nothing. Harvey Klein had some luck wrapping his head in cardboard with electrician's tape wound around it; that worked fairly well until his bike hit a bump and the eyeholes rotated so he couldn't see anything and he flew off the road and took out most of a pretty good stand of cucumbers with his face.

Even hockey was played without a helmet— which might explain the way many of the hockey players in my town talked. Or grunted.

Elbow and knee pads were nonexistent, except for hockey and football gear.

So, in our adventures in extreme sports, we were shredded and torn and road-rashed until it was hard to tell where road ended and boy began, and if there is one thing we all learned from this it was that if we'd had the safety gear we would have used it.

Oh, and of course that none of what we did should be done by anybody except heavily insured, highly trained professionals under adult supervision on closed courses with ambulances, doctors and MedEvac choppers standing by.

1

How Angel Peterson Got His Name

He is as old as me and that means he has had a life, has raised children and made a career and succeeded and maybe failed a few times and can look back on things, on old memories.

Carl Peterson—that's the name his mother and father gave him, but from the age of thirteen and for the rest of his life not a soul, not his wife or children or any friend has ever known him by that name.

He is always called Angel.

Angel Peterson, and I was there when he got his name.

■ ■ ■

We lived in northwestern Minnesota, up near the Canadian border and not far from the eastern border of North Dakota. The area is mostly cleared now and almost all farmland, but in the late forties and early fifties it was thickly forested and covered with small lakes and was perhaps the best hunting and fishing country in the world, absolutely crawling with fish and game. My friends and I spent most of our time in the woods, hunting, fishing or just camping, but we lived in town and had town lives as well.

Because the area was so remote, many farms still did not have electricity, nearly none had phones and the rare ones that did were on party lines, with all users on the same line so that anybody could listen in to anybody else (called rubbernecking). Individual phones were identified by the rings: two longs and a short ring would be one farm, two shorts and a long another farm and so forth. You would call somebody on a separate line by hand cranking a ringer on the side of your phone for the operator—one very long ring—and sticking his nose back in the power supply area of a console television set, trying to investigate the little crackling sounds and blue glow that came out of the ventilation holes. On his twelfth birthday, my pal Wayne Halverson licked the end of his finger and stuck it near the ventilation panel on his family's new RCA set. (Even though there was no television station programming to watch for nearly two more years they used it for a conversation piece and a place to put their bowling trophies, but my grandmother said the Halversons had always put on airs ever since Dewey, who was Wayne's great-great-grandfather, was kicked in the head by a workhorse and found that he could do accounting.)

Wayne never actually touched the top of the main rectifier tube and so didn't get the full jolt, which would have cooked him on the spot, but it arced over to his finger and a lesser charge, say enough to light two or three single-family dwellings for a week or so, slammed him back into the wall and left him unconscious for several min-

when she came on (it was always a woman) you would ask her to place your call, as in "Alice, I would like to talk to the Sunveldt farm over by Middle River," and the operator would ring them for you. Anybody on your own party line you would call by simply cranking their ring (my grandmother was a short, a long and a short).

In town we had private phones, with a clunky dial system that didn't always work, and that was about it.

There was—this is important—no television. There were just two channels in the major cities on the East and West Coasts. Almost nobody in town had a set. A TV set at that time was a huge buzzing, hissing black-and-white monster that had the added benefit of being dangerous. The coating on the inside of the picture tube required no less than forty-two *thousand* volts to operate, an amount that could easily kill fifteen or twenty horses. When television finally did come to the small towns up in Minnesota many a cat was turned into something close to a six-hundred-watt lightbulb by

utes. He later claimed that the incident was what made him the only one in our group who could actually talk to girls.

Radio was king and every Sunday night we would go to the Texaco station where Archie Swenson worked and listen to *Gunsmoke* on the radio. Matt Dillon (played by William Conrad in the radio version) would say things like "I'm marshal of Dodge City, Kansas. It's a chancy kind of job and makes a man watchful and a little bit lonely but somebody has to do it." Archie let us buy bottles of Coca-Cola for a nickel and bags of peanuts to put in the Cokes for another nickel and sit and listen to the radio as long as we didn't bother him at work and most especially if we didn't bother him if any older high school girls came by for gas or just to flirt with him. We were all twelve and thirteen and in Archie's world not quite human.

Archie was very, very cool. He was sixteen and had a perfect ducktail haircut and worked at the Texaco station full-time because he'd dropped out of school. He wore Levi's pulled so low that if he hadn't worn a T-shirt tucked in you would have seen the crack in his butt. He smoked and kept a pack of cigarettes rolled into the sleeve of his T-shirt and as boys we worshiped him, and also, much more important for the story of Angel Peterson, Archie had a car.

For the times, it was a very hot car. It was a '39 Ford sedan with an original V-8 engine and even though it was well over ten years old, with years of rough use during the Second World War, when small-town cars had to double as trucks and sometimes even tractors, even so it was a fast car. But more, Archie had "done things" to the car to make it faster. We were too ignorant to know how, but we were sure he had chopped this or enlarged that or channeled here and ported there to make it more powerful, and V-8 Fords were known for their speed. Some could do well over eighty miles an hour. We had read about some hot rods that would do a hundred miles an hour but dizzying speeds like that were usually only achieved on racetracks. Archie's car was also cool because he had a knob on the steering wheel that was made of clear Plexiglas and had a picture of a partially nude woman imbedded in it.

Two more things have to be understood about those long-ago times before the stage is finally set for Angel.

First, that part of northern Minnesota is completely and unbelievably flat. During successive ice ages, it was scoured flat by glaciers bulldozing their way south. When the glaciers melted, the land became an enormous inland freshwater sea called Lake Agassiz, which later receded to form the Great Lakes.

The land is so flat that if you cut down the trees and paved the area, you could probably roll a bowling ball from northern Minnesota to Montana without half trying.

Second, without television the only news, outside newspapers, came once a week at the theater matinee, when we would watch something called newsreels, short black-and-white film clips of the week's events.

And so in mid-January of 1954, when the Minnesota winter had settled its icy hand on the north country, it came to pass that four of us, all thirteen years old, went to a Saturday matinee showing of a really interesting and informative film about how radiation from nuclear testing (known then simply as A-Bomb experiments) had caused a species of common ant to mutate and grow to be huge, forty-foot-tall monsters. The radiation also made the ants develop an overwhelming need to eat human flesh. The movie was called *Them!* and we all agreed it was well worth the fifteen cents' admission and the extra dime for popcorn and another nickel for a box of Dots.

We were also impressed by how the giant ants, which made a sound strangely similar to small, peeping chicks, could suck all the flesh from a cow's skeleton (or a human's, come to that) and leave the bones intact. As we exited the theater, we argued about how *we* would have handled the ants. As I remember it, the government invaded their nests and very brave men attacked them with flamethrowers. . . .

That is, we all discussed the film except Carl Peterson. He had been strangely quiet since the showing of the newsreel and a short sports film about a man who had gone for the world speed record on skis and exceeded seventy-four miles an hour.

We walked along in the steam from our breath, talking about giant ants that sucked flesh from bones, and Carl stopped dead and said,

"I can do it."

"Do what?" Pete Amundsen asked.

"Break the speed record on skis."

There was a pause. Then, from Pete: "Here? There isn't a hill for a thousand miles—maybe two thousand. How are you going to get up any speed?"

Carl shook his head. "I don't need a hill. It didn't say anything about a hill. It just said you have to go fast on skis. Well, I've got these old army trooper skis and we can smooth them up."

"I don't care how smooth they are, on flat ground they won't move—"

"Archie," Carl cut in. "We get Archie to pull me

with his car. He's got a hot car, hasn't he? We just get him to pull me faster than seventy-four miles an hour and bingo, I've got the record." And then he said the one thing he should never have said.

"It can't miss—what can go wrong?"

Every single one of us knew at least one very good reason not to do it—it would break the skis; it would break the car; it would break Carl; it would *kill* Carl. But not one of us said a word.

In all of us was the thirst for what can only be called scientific knowledge, the need to know the answer to the question:

What exactly *would* happen to Carl if he went over seventy-four miles an hour on a pair of army surplus skis?

Of course, there were many logistical problems to be overcome. Carl had the skis, that was true, but the rest of the equipment was lacking.

Nowadays, it may be hard to realize how difficult it was then to get simple things for outdoor use. There was no L.L.Bean or any other specific outdoor supplier. There was the Sears and Roebuck catalog, and they would send you a shotgun or a tent that the famous baseball player Ted Williams said was the best in the world.

There really wasn't much in the way of equipment available anyway, nor were there any real sporting goods stores. Hardware stores sometimes sold roller skates with metal wheels that locked on to your shoes with clamps. Ammunition for .22 rifles was sold in grocery stores.

Which left army surplus.

The Second World War had just ended nine years earlier and clothing, rations, ammo, guns, jeeps, even some explosives could be bought for almost nothing from the government. A 30/06 rifle went for seventeen dollars, a .45 automatic pistol was eleven dollars, a jeep cost a hundred, a fighter plane went for three hundred and you could even buy a tank or a battleship. It was said that John Wayne had bought a destroyer or minesweeper and turned it into a yacht, and there was a bachelor farmer out east of town who bought a hundred or more *tons* of high explosives to use for clearing stumps. (It didn't work out so well for him because he'd stored them in his barn and as near as they could figure it a mouse or rat chewed on a blasting cap and set them off, making the whole farm vanish. The crater smoked for days. All they found of the farmer was his left boot but Archie said that didn't prove much because it could have been anybody's foot in the boot.)

So we went to the army surplus store and for seven dollars and eighty-one cents we completely outfitted Carl for his world-record speed-skiing attempt. For those who might think we weren't serious about his effort, let me point out that this was not an inconsiderable sum. A man working in a factory was paid a dollar and five cents an hour and a Dairy Queen cone was a nickel—ten cents if it was dipped in chocolate.

By pooling all our money we spent nearly a man's daily wages on Carl. We got him the best equipment we could find.

We found flight goggles—the kind with the large, soft rubber wraparound frame—and a leather flight helmet. A leather flight jacket used up four dollars; it was on sale because it had three holes that were kind of stained. We did not say the jacket might bring him bad luck even though some of us were thinking it.

Then came sheepskin flight pants, only half a foot too long, sheepskin-lined flight boots just two sizes too large and a jumbo pair of genuine sheepskin gunner's mittens with a separate trigger finger.

When Carl was fully dressed, standing there in Bruce Carlson's garage, he looked like a large leather ball with tinted green eyes.

"It must have taken four or five sheep to make his outfit," Bruce said.

"I can't see through the goggles," Carl said. "Should they be all fogged up like this?"

"Don't worry," Bruce said. "Once you're outside and moving in back of Archie's car they'll clear right up."

"Should the pants legs be bunched like that around my ankles?"

"Don't worry," Bruce said. "Once you're outside and moving, the wind will tighten them up."

"Should the jacket be this loose around my neck?"

"Don't worry," Bruce said. "Once you're outside and moving . . ."

And so, with all Carl's worries completely covered, we walked down to the Texaco station and approached the second most important ingredient in the record attempt: Archie.

"No," he said. "Absolutely not."

He was adamant until Bruce said, "We'll give you five dollars."

We all looked at each other, then gave Bruce the evil eye. *What* five dollars?

"Cash?" Archie asked.

Bruce nodded.

"In advance?"

Silence.

Pete finally said, "As soon as we've made it shoveling walks after the next snow ..."

Archie thought a moment. He probably knew we didn't have that much ready money, knew we had spent what we had on Carl's clothes. He also knew we would pay him. Not paying a debt to Archie—Archie of the ducktail haircut and hot car, who was said to sometimes carry a switchblade, *that* Archie—would be something close to suicide for a thirteen-year-old.

He shrugged. "All right—but you pay me right after the next snow."

We were standing in Alan Grenville's garage because Bruce's parents were home and we didn't want anyone to notice us. Carl was suited up. We had opened the garage to let the cold air in—it was fifteen below zero outside—so Carl wouldn't overheat, but he looked a bit sweaty just the same. I thought it might be nerves and he might back out.

"You don't have to do this," Alan said, as

though reading my mind. Still, I had that healthy scientific curiosity about just exactly what would happen to Carl.

We all turned to look at Alan and Carl. Alan's mother was Canadian and that made him some-how more sensible and wiser than the rest of us. Canadians were known to be smarter because they had better schools and even though Alan had been born in the States and had never actually lived in Canada, he had a certain status.

"You can back out now with no shame."

Alan always sounded so...so *official,* maybe because he had some of his mother's accent. He actually said that: "No shame." Just like a Mountie would say, I thought.

But Carl shook his head. "No. I want that record. Call Archie. Now." He looked out the garage door at the Friday evening light. "We still have a couple of hours before dark."

But it turned out that Archie wouldn't be able to make the run until the next day, which was probably better because it was Saturday and we'd have more time. So I slept over at Carl's house and we spent the night getting his gear ready.

Of course it was as ready as it could be but we kept going over it. Then Carl brought up the fact that he hadn't waxed his skis. I'm pretty sure it was Carl because I don't want to be the one who said it, because everybody later agreed that waxing the skis the way we did might have been where the problems started.

I had heard of waxing skis somewhere but Carl had seen a picture taken in Norway in a *National Geographic* magazine when he was looking for purely educational pictures of naked women in Africa or South America. In this picture some Norwegians were waxing their skis.

"It said the wax made their skis faster."

"We don't have any wax," I pointed out.

"Mom does. Her canning paraffin. She's got tons of it."

Everybody canned vegetables and fruit in the fall and they poured wax over the top of the jars to seal them airtight. One of the best things in the world was opening a new jar of chokecherry jelly, because the wax had been poured in hot and the jelly had mixed into it as it hardened, so you could chew on the wax and taste the jelly for hours. It was better than candy.

We found the wax and I held a cake of it and one ski, and he had another cake and the other ski. "How do we put it on?" I asked.

"Rub it back and forth on the wood until it warms up and then it should stick."

So we rubbed, and rubbed, and just when I thought it wouldn't work, the wood actually warmed and the wax became sticky and almost seemed to flow onto the surface of the ski.

"How much?" I asked.

He shrugged. "Wipe it all on. The more the better."

And so we did. Each ski had on it what amounted to a good quarter of a pound of wax, nearly a quarter of an inch thick along its full length, and when we leaned the skis against the outside wall of the house and went to bed the last thing Carl said to me as I curled up on the floor in a sleeping bag was:

"Man, those things ought to be fast."

We didn't know that there was special ski wax, that some waxes made the ski faster and some slower for climbing hills. We didn't know that paraffin was most decidedly *not* good ski wax and that when the temperature was zero or below, paraffin actually gripped the snow.

The next morning we walked a block and a half to meet Archie at ten o'clock behind Erickson's grocery, out of sight of any houses because most parents didn't exactly approve of Archie. And it was a sure bet that if Carl's mother or father saw him leaving the house dressed exactly like a World War II bomber pilot ready for combat with a pair of skis over one shoulder and a coil of nylon parachute cord over the other and saw him get into Archie's hot car, they might ask embarrassing questions and actually might not approve of Carl's going for the world speed record on skis—parents being notoriously shortsighted about such things. As we made our way to meet Archie, Carl smiled. He seemed confident.

"It's a great day for it," he said, looking up at the clear blue sky. There were ice crystals in the air because it was at least twenty below. "Perfect . . ."

Archie was grumpy. It was early for him and he'd had trouble getting the car started because of the cold, and the heater hadn't fully started cooking yet.

But the five dollars loomed higher than his objections, since he only made seventy-five cents an hour working at the Texaco. Wayne and Alan soon showed up. Wayne was bundled so thickly his body was almost invisible. Alan smiled and held up a small Brownie camera, the kind you had to look down through from the top.

"I thought I'd get a picture right when you break the record," Alan said, and nobody smiled.

It had to be said of Archie that once he made a decision he was in for the whole ride.

"We'll head out east of town, along that drainage ditch that runs past all that old swampland beyond those farms," he said as we all packed into the car. Three of us sat in back while Carl and Archie sat in front. Archie had tied the skis to the side with some of Carl's parachute cord.

As he drove, he said, "It's flat for miles out there and except for the crossroads, which are iced over, it should give us a great place for the run."

"Good," Carl said. He said only one word, and he was the only one speaking. Alan and I were busy with our own thoughts. Wayne was sitting in back of Archie and was trying to turn his head upside down and see the woman in the steering wheel knob, which was a waste because she was just a blur and you couldn't see her even if you closed one eye and squinted, and usually Archie had his hand over her anyway.

It took about half an hour to get out along the ditch, which was really more of a shallow depression that had been installed to drain hundreds of square miles of swamp and make farmland. The ditch itself was nearly twenty miles long.

At every mile a road crossed the ditch and led

back to one of the farms scattered here and there. When we'd passed four of the roads and found each one of them iced over, Archie stopped the car. "This is as good a place as any to start. How do you want to do this?"

We all turned and looked at Carl. He was looking away from us, in front of the car, down the long ditch, which stretched to the horizon. It was full of snow and nearly level with the road, with small ripple-drifts from the wind that blew across the huge open area. Where the snow in the ditch came up to each small crossroad, there was only a slight bump, then ten feet or so of icy snow on the road and then a slight bump back down into the ditch.

"How do you want to do this?" Archie repeated. "I have to work this afternoon."

We had planned it and talked about it most of the night. Carl nodded and said softly, "I'll get in the ditch and we'll tie the rope to the back bumper. You start slow and pick it up until you get to seventy-five miles an hour." He stopped and looked at Archie, a new authority in his voice. "Will your car do seventy-five?"

Normally this would have constituted a grave insult, but Archie only nodded. "She'll do better than that."

Carl smiled. "That's all I want. The man in the newsreel did just over seventy-four. If we do seventy-five I'll have the record."

The way he said it, so clean and simple and straightforward, he made it sound as if it would be a walk in the park. Carl clumped into the ditch on the skis and we tied one end of the parachute cord to the bumper and Archie ran the car a hundred feet down the gravel road, driving on the left so he'd be close to the ditch, and we handed the other end of the rope to Carl.

He tied a double knot at the end so it wouldn't slip out of his hands and then lined himself up in the middle of the ditch and nodded.

"All right. Let's go."

Archie let the clutch out carefully, eased it out until the rope was tight, looked back, saw Carl nod and started out.

Carl fell flat on his face and let go of the rope.

With the thick paraffin wax binding to the cold snow, the skis didn't move at all.

"The skis are stuck," he said, getting up. "I think it's the wax." He thought a moment and then said, "All right. I'll tie a loop in the rope around my wrist so I won't let go. You start slow and I'll lean back until the wax is rubbed off, then you go faster and faster until we break the record."

Archie looked at him, then shrugged. "We'll need a signal. Some way for you to tell us when you're ready to go faster."

"I'll hold up my thumb when I want you to go faster, hold it down when I want you to slow down." Carl demonstrated with the big gunner's mitts and the thumb stood up, easily seen.

"I'll watch for the signal," I said.

"I'll be ready with the camera," Wayne said. He had the camera because he was sitting in the backseat on the same side as the ditch.

"I'll be ready to give first aid," Alan said.

Archie said nothing but coolly got back in the car.

And for a second or two it seemed as if it might

work. Archie let the clutch out, Carl leaned back and wrapped the rope around his wrist and the rope tightened and Carl started to move.

Slowly at first, as the wax first smeared, then scraped off his skis. I watched carefully as the load came onto the rope and the stretch came out of it and Carl's thumb was pointed straight up.

"Faster," I hollered over the noise of the wind. I had the window open so I could see better. "He wants to go faster!"

"Thirty miles an hour," Archie yelled. "No, thirty-five, now forty..."

I squinted. Some snow blew up off the road, obscuring Carl a bit, but then it cleared as the speed increased and I could see him better.

"More speed!" I cried. "His thumb is still up."

"He seems," Alan said, sounding exactly like a Mountie, "to be in complete control of his situation."

"Fifty!" Archie yelled. "Fifty-five..."

I glanced quickly out of the corner of my eye to see if Wayne had the camera ready but he was looking at the steering wheel knob and as I watched he raised the camera and tried to take a picture of it.

"Wayne!" I bellowed. "Get ready!"

Then I looked back at Carl. He was really moving now, the skis cleaned off and the rope taut. And Alan seemed to be right, Carl was in control. We came upon the first crossroad and Carl leaned back, looking for all the world like a professional water-skier: He slapped the skis up over the small bump, slid cleanly over the icy road and dropped neatly into the ditch on the other side.

"Sixty!" Archie screamed. "Sixty-one, -two, -three . . ."

I looked into the ditch and through the wind and snow and I thought now that perhaps things weren't going as smoothly as I had thought. The goggles were tinted but still I could see that Carl's eyes looked larger—they seemed to fill the goggles. Maybe we should begin to slow the car down a bit.

But the thumb was still pointed up, straight up, wonderfully and courageously up, and I nodded at Carl, marveling at his bravery.

"He wants to go for it!" I slapped Archie on the shoulder, something I never would have done before then. You didn't touch Archie. But to illustrate the intensity of the moment, Archie didn't seem to notice. Instead he nodded and yelled, "I didn't believe the little bugger had it in him!" and floored the pedal.

The Ford seemed to leap ahead.

"Seventy!" Archie screamed. "Seventy-one, -two, -five, -six . . . he's got it! He's got the record!"

I waved out the window at Carl and gave him the thumbs-up signal. But he didn't seem to notice. He was in a semicrouch, one arm holding the rope and the other waving, or trying to wave as the wind slapped it down and back like a rag.

"Oooohhhhhhh!" Carl screamed. I couldn't believe it. He was yelling *"Goooooo!"* The thumb was still straight up—he wanted to go faster!

"Eighty." Archie shook his head. "That's all I can get—eighty-two and a half miles an hour!"

And then it happened.

I turned and looked ahead and saw to my

horror that we were coming up to the next cross-road and that the grader had been there and planed the icy snow down.

It was bare gravel.

And before I could think or say anything Carl bumped over the small snow bump next to the road and landed at almost exactly eighty-two and a half miles an hour in the middle of the gravel.

We would learn that somewhere early on in the run, after approximately thirty-five miles an hour, Carl realized that he had made a terrible mistake and that he did not want to go any faster, did not want to try to break the record and most emphatically did not want to go to eighty-two and a half miles an hour.

He had tried to scream, had bellowed, *"No!"* but all we heard was "Ooooohhhh!" The rest was torn away by the wind.

He had tried to wave but the wind just knocked his arm down and on a bump the rope went slack and then tightened and caught his right arm around the wrist so he couldn't get it loose, couldn't signal with that arm either. And then, because the speed gods had apparently taken over his life and *they* wanted to see him break the record—as Wayne said—or because he was just plain unlucky—as Alan said—or because he was dumb as a fence post—as Archie said—the same loop that caught his wrist had snagged the right thumb on his flight mitten, jerked it off his thumb and twisted it in such a way as to make the empty mitten thumb stand straight in the air, as if Carl wanted to go faster and faster. . . .

But for now, we watched in awe.

The skis stopped dead.

Stopped dead when they hit the gravel and Carl skipped out of them like a rock across the top of a pond—that is, if the rock weighed a hundred and thirty-five pounds and if it were made out of flesh and blood encased in sheepskin and if it were being towed by a car at over eighty miles an hour, and if the water were snow and ice.

Wayne was still looking at the steering wheel knob and Alan had turned for a moment to look at the road, this being the first time he had ever gone over eighty miles an hour.

But I was watching Carl, looking for his signal. For a second he reminded me of a swordfish I'd seen in a newsreel that had jumped out of the water and was trying to shake the hook out of its mouth.

Carl did not hit the gravel road, which was a miracle because it would probably have killed him. Instead when the skis stopped he seemed to spring into the air, clearing the rest of the road and flying into the snow on the other side, burrowing in for half a second or so, then exploding out, almost vertical, his hands twisting like the swordfish's head as he tried to rip himself loose from the rope.

He failed. At the height of his arc the rope snapped tight at eighty miles an hour and snaked him back under the snow, where for two heartbeats he looked for all the world like a high-speed gopher. We couldn't see him at all, just this rippling little bulge of snow, and then he burst forth into the open again.

You notice funny things in an emergency. I saw that his thumb was still pointed straight up and I thought, Man, Carl is one brave guy. He doesn't even care if he's got skis on, he's still going for it.

"Stop the car!"

It was Alan. He had turned and seen what was happening and had more presence of mind than me—everything had happened so fast that I hadn't had much time to react. And, to be honest, I still had that great curiosity. Carl's thumb was still pointed up and who was I to deny him fame?

Archie hit the brakes as soon as he heard Alan scream—hit them so hard that Wayne flew over the backseat and planted his face on the steering wheel knob, which gave him a black eye we talked about for years.

Unfortunately the brakes on the Ford worked better than the snow's friction on Carl and when the car stopped, he had the great misfortune to pass us, although he had stopped burrowing into drifts like a gopher. As he passed, he flopped end over end and Archie said later that he'd looked like a dead carp.

He lay ahead of us in the ditch, unmoving, a lump of snow and mangled sheepskin, and we piled out of the car and ran to him.

Floundered to him, really, because the snow in the ditch was soft (which had probably saved his life). We sank into it up to our waists.

"Carl!" Alan yelled, leaning over him. "Can you hear me?"

Nothing.

But Wayne, who was holding a hand over his eye, said, "There's life! I saw his hand move."

Then an arm came up, just half an inch, fell back, and a muffled voice said, "Snow . . ."

"What?" Alan asked, leaning over to hear better. "What did you say?"

"Snow," came the mumble, ". . . too much snow."

We pulled him up out of the ditch and found he was absolutely right. There was too much snow. It had been driven under his eyelids; it filled his mouth, was packed in his ears and jammed inside his jacket; it filled his pants, was packed into every opening and crevice of his clothes and his body; and as we stripped him in the car and shook the snow out on the road and helped him to get dressed again in the wet clothes, he never said a word. Not one word, until we were driving back to look for the skis (we only found one) and headed for town to get Carl to his house and into a warm bath.

He sat huddled and silent in the back, even when Archie paid him the supreme compliment of saying, "You got balls, kid. You broke the record."

Nothing, no sign Carl had even heard Archie. Then, as we crossed the Eighth Street Bridge and started into town, he raised his head and said:

"I heard the angels sing."

"What?" I said.

"I said I heard the angels sing. Right at the worst part, when I went under the first time, I heard the angels sing."

"Oh. That's nice." All right, I thought, maybe he took a pretty good shot in the head. We couldn't find the flight helmet either, or the goggles. Maybe he thinks the angels were singing for him.

But it was Alan, who had that presence of mind, it was Alan who asked in his best Mountie voice, "What were they singing?"

Carl looked out the side window of the car at nothing, at everything. "They were singing 'Your Cheatin' Heart,' by Hank Williams."

And after that nobody ever called him anything but Angel Peterson.

2

The Miracle of Flight

Nobody had flown by human power then and private air travel had not advanced very much because of the Second World War. It was only nine years after the end of that war, and we were just past the Korean conflict, so most aviation research was done on military aircraft.

There were no jet airliners. There were military jets that had fought in Korea, but commercial air travel was still in lumbering two- and four-engine prop planes. Some airlines still used the old DC-3s for passenger service on short hops (incredibly, now, more than fifty years later, some small airlines *still* use those same old DC-3s) and they cruised a little over a hundred knots, about the speed some people drive their Mercedes on the L.A. freeways. Fast for a car, but very slow for an airliner.

People had learned to glide, though. There were gliding clubs all over the country and more in Europe, but there was no such thing as a hang glider, or even the concept of one.

Until Emil (pronounced "Eee-mull") learned to fly. And after he did, like Angel, he was never the same again, although I think the fact that Emil later became a mortician and ultimately had to get out of the business because it was rumored he was selling body parts to collectors (*collectors?*) had nothing to do with Emil's accidental discovery of hang gliding.

Emil's real problem, or what would prove to be a problem, was that he was what folks called "tight with a nickel."

He was so tight that I once saw him buy a candy bar, eat half of it and then sell the remaining half to another boy in school for the full five cents the original candy bar cost. Six times in one day. This doesn't say much about the six boys who bought the half-bars, or about Emil's ethics, but it shows how far he would go to stretch a nickel. Actually, I was one of the boys who bought half a candy bar but in my defense it was late in the afternoon in history class, which was taught by the football coach, who related every aspect of history to football ("Caesar would have made a good quarterback.... Cleopatra would have made a good quarterback, if she had been a man.... Napoleon would have made a good quarterback.... Robert E. Lee would have made a good quarterback....") and who had the most monotonous voice on the planet. When Emil offered me the half candy bar, I would have given him a dollar if he'd asked for it, I was that bored.

And in Emil's defense it must be added that money did not come easy in those days. Most jobs for a young boy were hard work and many were downright dangerous.

During the late summer and early fall it was

possible to get work on the farms around town. There were no safety regulations then or child labor laws and the farm work could be crippling. I worked one farm for a summer when I was twelve and the work was seven days a week, fourteen hours a day for a dollar and a half a day (not an hour but a *day*) and food and a bed to collapse in.

In the fall it was possible to get temporary employment picking potatoes but this was no picnic either. A large machine went down the rows and dug the potatoes up and we crawled on our hands and knees behind and picked up the potatoes by hand.

For a whopping seven cents a bushel.

In the winter there was school and no real part-time work for us except selling newspapers in the bars, delivering newspapers to homes in the morning and setting pins in the bowling alley at night and on weekends. Or, in my case, all three.

Nobody I knew got an allowance. My parents were pretty much the town drunks and I didn't get any help from them in any situation, let alone financial. But even with my friends who had decent parents, any extra money for school clothes or just for spending had to come from work. In 1955, when I was sixteen, I hitchhiked three hundred miles to get a job at a Birds Eye fresh-frozen vegetable plant for the harvest in southern Minnesota and received the truly astounding wage of a dollar and five cents an hour—eight dollars and forty cents for an eight-hour day. It was what a man made to support a family, truly a fortune for a young boy.

But when we were twelve and thirteen, there was no money like that, and anything that was relatively expensive became very dear.

I remember buying my first bow and materials to make a dozen arrows: eight field points and four broadheads, with a fletcher to put the feathers on, which I got at the small meatpacking plant from turkeys being taken in to slaughter. The bow was a Fred Bear Cub and cost thirty-nine dollars and I had it on layaway at the hardware store for four and a half months before I had enough to pay for it.

So for somebody who was already very tight with money, like Emil, every dime was important. It was strange, then, that Emil would be the one to make the investment that allowed him to become the first person to try hang gliding. . . .

Of course it didn't start out as Emil trying to fly. Once again, it began with the army surplus store.

During the Second World War there were no synthetic fabrics, and parachutes were made of silk. It was a low-grade silk to be sure, but after the war the material in the parachutes was in great demand by women who used it to make clothing, because silk was very expensive. Many different-sized parachutes, full size for men and smaller sizes for light freight or mortar flares, were for sale in the surplus stores.

Before Emil got in on the act, Willy Parnell took a small freight parachute to the top of the water tower, where he unintentionally invented base jumping. Actually, base plummeting might be more accurate, since the parachute he used was for something that weighed eighty pounds and Willy came in at a hundred and sixteen. He said he thought it was working, though the ground seemed to be coming up pretty fast, until he went through the roof of the Carlsons' chicken coop. The article in the paper was headlined:

BOY CRASHES COOP!

The story said Mrs. Carlson wasn't sure if the chickens would ever lay again, since, as she said, "They have a powerful fear of hawks and they thought it was a giant hawk that come after them."

Several of the chickens and a goodly pile of chicken manure combined to break Willy's fall and keep him from killing himself but he did manage to break his right ankle and missed out on some school and all gym classes for the rest of the year, and he got the nickname of Stinky Parnell because of the way the chicken manure ground into his skin—the smell didn't go away right at first.

Which had nothing to do with Emil and how he invented hang gliding.

It all started because Emil's mother sent him to the army surplus to get a parachute. Emil's older sister was going to the prom and her mother wanted to make a silk dress for her. She had called the order in to the store and paid for it and Emil was supposed to just stop and pick it up.

Which was when he saw the target kite.

During the Second World War, planes, even fighters, rarely went much over four hundred miles an hour—compared to the two thousand or so miles an hour they do now—and there was no such thing as a missile. American fighter planes used wing-mounted machine guns and they had to fly tight on an opponent's tail and open on him from close range, under two hundred yards.

New fighter pilots were trained on target kites made of silk with aluminum frames and a silhouette of an enemy Japanese Zero Fighter, top view, in black with the famous red meatballs on the wings. The kite would be flown far above a target range on parachute cord, and new pilots would

make passes at it and shoot it down without en-
dangering the pilot of a tow plane because of their
inexperience.

The kites were well made and very large, eight
feet wide by ten or twelve feet long, usually a pale
blue so the kite body would disappear against the
sky and only the silhouette of the plane would
show.

And there was one on the wall of the army surplus store when Emil went in to pick up the parachute for his mother.

He had to have it.

"I don't know why," he told us later. "I never
thought of it before. It was just there on the wall,
blue and black with those red meatballs, and I had
to have it."

And it was expensive.

Eleven dollars.

Emil tried his best to get cranky old Phillips,
the man who owned the surplus store, to come off
the price. But Phillips knew he had Emil and stuck
to his guns. Emil paid in full.

Which was not just eleven dollars; it was setting

a hundred lines of league bowling. Or selling two hundred and twenty newspapers in bars at a nickel profit a paper, when on an average night you were lucky to sell ten. Or shoveling twenty-one walks and driveways after a heavy snow.

And still he had to have it, and the amount that it cost him, in life's blood, in effort, in *money,* was the reason for the near disaster.

At first he decided he would just hang the kite on the wall in his room.

"...But it just about covered the whole wall," he said later, "and I would lie there at night looking at it in the moonlight, thinking of what it was, what it was for, and I knew what I had to do. I would have to fly the kite."

And that is where we came in. With something as big as the target kite you couldn't just go out and fly it. He would need help to get it in the air and so on an early summer Saturday Emil showed up at Wayne's house on his bicycle with the kite disassembled and rolled up, and a ball of perhaps two hundred yards of thin parachute cord. He nodded to us and nobody needed to speak.

We all got on our bikes and followed him out east of town, near the same area where Angel had broken the speed record on skis, to the large open spaces along the drainage ditches where there was room for something as big as the target kite.

We had all flown kites, mostly those we'd made ourselves from plans in *Boys' Life* magazine. I'd even tried to make a four-foot-long wing kite and had come close to flying it before it crashed and broke.

But we'd never tried anything this big. Still, as Alan pointed out, the principle was the same.

"We lay the cord out on the ground, Emil holds on to this end, we carry the kite down and shove it up in the air to get it started and Emil hangs on. Wayne, maybe you'd better stay with Emil and hang on with him. The wind is picking up and it might take two of you to hold it."

The wind *was* picking up a bit, but it didn't seem

that strong. Even so, when we had bolted the kite to-gether it took both Alan and me just to keep it flat.

On the front of the kite was a heavy-duty bri-dle and there were three different points where you could attach the rope.

"I don't know," Emil confessed. "What do you think?" He turned to Alan.

"It seems like the top attachment would let the kite fly a little flatter when it gets up and take some of the load off."

"All right. Let's hook it there."

Alan was a Boy Scout and knew knots and he attached the parachute line with some kind of double-whammy-sheepshank killer knot that would never come loose and at the other end of the line Emil tied a two-foot piece of hockey stick drilled with holes for the rope to go through.

"So I'll have a handle," he said. "I don't want to lose her."

I confess that right then I had a series of men-tal images featuring Emil, thin, not overly tall, holding the wooden bar and the kite, wide, big—

huge—catching the rising wind. I must further confess that I had a similar scientific curiosity to that which I'd had right before Carl broke the speed record on skis—just what *would* happen to Emil when the wind caught the kite?—but I didn't want to dampen Emil's enthusiasm so I said nothing.

We were at last ready, with Alan and me walking downwind from Wayne and Emil two hundred yards, holding the kite flat and parallel to the ground, and the cord lined out down the road. This was difficult now that the wind was picking up. We looked back and saw Emil and Wayne holding the handle and Emil waved and nodded and yelled something that I didn't quite get but he told us later that it was "Let her go!"

And we did. Well, not quite. We didn't have that much control. We turned the kite's target face to the wind and raised the front edge so the wind could get under the kite, and it simply left us.

I have never seen anything like it. There was a popping sound, Alan and I were both knocked back on our butts, and then a kind of *rip-rippl*ing hiss as the kite shot up into the heavens, dragging the line up with it. In seconds it lifted Wayne and Emil slightly from the ground, swinging them down the road toward us.

There was a moment then, a couple of seconds when we still had some control. The wind had freshened considerably and the line to the kite, attached to the top of the bridle, made the kite head up until it was pulling almost vertically on the two boys. Together Emil and Wayne were just a bit too heavy for the kite, even though it was pulling straight up, and with the wind starting to snap a bit, they achieved a kind of equilibrium.

For a moment.

Then two things happened. The order in which they happened would forever be a subject of controversy with us.

A strong gust of wind caught the kite and jerked on the line.

And Wayne let go of the handle.

For the rest of his life since, Wayne has said that the gust jerked the handle out of his hand.

Emil swears that Wayne let go before the gust came. And that he smiled when he let go.

Whatever. The results were the same.

There was a *whuff*ing sound from the sky as the gust hit the kite, and a small scream as Emil realized what was happening. Quicker than anybody could think, Emil was gone with the kite.

Legends are born this way. Willy jumping off the water tower with a small freight parachute to invent base jumping, Angel with that mitten thumb sticking up and Emil hanging from the hockey stick handle as the kite dragged him into the sky.

There were lengthy arguments later about just exactly how high he went and how long he flew. But none of us had a watch or knew how to measure height.

These things happened: The target kite found a kind of balance, lifted on the wind and flew as a sort of glider for an extended period.

Emil said it felt like several hours and it almost pulled his arms out of their sockets, but that, of course, was silly.

Certainly it was several minutes. Wayne thought ten or so; Alan, who was always careful, thought at least seven. I'm sure it was close to fifteen.

It was a very long time to hang on to a piece of old hockey stick.

As for height, Emil cleared a stand of old oak trees near the Larson farm that were over eighty feet tall.

By the time he cleared the oaks he had gone more than a mile and he had been both higher and lower and then higher again than the oaks, and higher than the Larsons' silo, and higher than the Larsons' barn, and higher than the Larsons' granary, and was almost directly over the Larsons' straw pile when he decided it was time to abandon ship and he let go of the hockey stick.

Farms then used threshing machines rather than combines to harvest their grain, which meant they brought the grain in shocks to the farm and fed them through the machines and blew all the straw into huge piles, usually near the barn where it could be used for animal bedding through the winter. These piles were sometimes higher than the barn itself, and it was over the straw pile that Emil decided to bail out.

"I didn't panic," he said, "at least not then. I looked down, saw the straw, looked up and saw the kite—the blue had disappeared and it looked like I was being hauled by a Japanese Zero—and I let go."

Unfortunately the straw was old and had lost some of its softness and equally unfortunately Emil did not hit square on the top of the pile but on the side, about halfway down.

On the side nearest the pigpen.

We had been running after him, screaming useless advice: "Don't let go!" "Let go!" "Don't let go!" And, from Wayne, "Can you see town from up there?" We arrived nearby just as he let go.

"Oh, man, he's going to hit the straw pile," Wayne said, and, with a resounding *whummph!*, Emil seemed to settle into the straw for a beat, then bounced up in a perfect arc and augered into the mud in the middle of the pigpen.

Something most people don't know about pigs is that they're really clean animals. They pick one corner of their pen for a toilet and they always use that corner. That is, for the solids. For the wetter part they go everywhere.

Emil was lucky in that he missed the corner that was the pigs' toilet.

But pigs love mud, and they root up the dirt and mix it with slop and waste in the middle of the pen until it's a regular quagmire of mulched mud maybe two feet deep. Here Emil came to rest with a great *thwoooock*ing sound, head down, tail up, scaring the pigs so badly they tore down the entire back fence and ran to the house looking for help.

The Larsons did not have a water pressure system and so no hose was available, but there was a small stock tank in back of the barn and Emil climbed in, clothes and all, and sloshed around until we could stand to be near him.

Then it took us an hour to round up the hogs and fix the pen with Mrs. Larson, whose husband was in town. She kindly brought us sandwiches and glasses of buttermilk before we got our bikes and headed back home.

She seemed to take it all in stride when we explained how the kite had taken Emil over the barn and silo and into the hog pen and I thought that was strange until she smiled gently and said:

"My boy is grown and gone now, off to be a doctor in the city. But he was like you. Just the same as. I once saw him try to fly from the granary to the barn with nothing but some feed sacks and sticks for wings."

Emil wanted to go look for the kite but we'd seen it blow higher and higher when he dropped off, out over the wilderness of the great Oak Leaf Swamp, where it was all peat bogs and thick weeds. It was gone for good.

He sighed, pedaling along. In back of us. *Well* in back of us. He smelled worse than Willy in the chicken coop. "I'm sure going to miss that kite."

And I thought, I'll bet—it almost killed you. But, just as he had with Carl, it was Alan who thought to ask the right question:

"Why didn't you let go when Wayne let go? Why did you keep hanging on?"

He said nothing for a moment, just pedaling; then he sighed. "I thought about it. Just for a second."

"Then why didn't you?"

"Alan," he said, as if talking to an idiot, "the thing cost me eleven dollars. A man hates to let go of that much money."

3

Orvis Orvisen and the Crash and Bash

There are boys' names that you know will make a boy popular and successful and cool and able to talk to girls (more on this later) and will make him have a wonderful life and probably get rich and marry a cheerleader and have a hot car....

Clint is such a name, and perhaps Steve, although not necessarily Steven, and Brad, and maybe best of all Nick. You just know that somebody named Nick is going to get it all.

And then there are the other names:

Harvey, maybe, and Sidney and Gary and Wesley—names that connote, well, not necessarily a loser, in fact not at all a loser, but somebody who you know is going to have to work that little bit harder to make it all happen for him.

A boy stands up in the back of a new class and says, "Hello, my name is Harvey Hemesvedt"—not Harv, or Sid or Wes, but the whole name, Harvey— you just *know* that kid is going to be busy for a while.

And if a boy's last name is Orvisen, and his parents are silly or addled or just plain cruel enough to give him the first name of Orvis so he has to say, "Hello, my name is Orvis Orvisen," they might as well just rub him with raw liver and throw him into a pit of starving wolves.

And if you take the same Orvis Orvisen and put him not in a public school but in a Catholic school, where all the boys play hockey—sometimes with live pucks if they can find a chicken or a cat—and think fighting almost to the death is a form of recreation . . .

Well, Orvis had a tough row to hoe.

"I barely made it home alive from my first day of school," he told me when I met him. "They wanted to play catch with me—not with a ball, but throw *me* back and forth. Man, they were worse than the nuns."

We had all heard horror stories about the nuns who taught at the Catholic school, how they used yardsticks like broadswords and dipped the edges in salt so they would hurt more and didn't care if you bled as long as you didn't drip on the floor. Whenever I had seen nuns they always seemed quiet and almost nice, but there were Catholic boys who were so mean they scared bad dogs, and these boys would cross the street and hide in back of a garbage can in terror when they saw Sister Eunicia walking by.

And so Orvis came to be better and tougher than all of us combined, and so Orvis became the one who tried the Circle of Death.

But first, a bit more about him.

Somewhere along in the seventh grade Orvis evolved a novel method of self-defense. He would evaluate his difficulty, consider what was going to happen to him and then do it to himself.

It was brilliant in its simplicity. If, for instance, a group of boys were going to stick him in his locker—something that happened to him so often, he told me he was going to make an emergency pack with a flashlight and some food and water for when he had to stay in there for longer periods—he would just run to his locker, climb in and slam the door behind himself.

"That way I can control the damage. I thought of numbering the different types of punishment to make it easier for the bullies. They really aren't very bright, you know. I'd just give them a list with the numbers and torture on it. So the locker would be one, and jerking my own underwear into a wedgie would be two, all the way down to going headfirst into a garbage can for seventeen or eighteen, and maybe twenty-two for being pantsed in front of the girls' locker room. That way when I see them coming they could just yell a number and I could do it to myself."

Well, it worked, and it made him tough. Later, a lot later, when he finally decided it was time to stand up to them, he caught Bobby Bunnis, one of the worst bullies, in back of the hockey rink and beat him so hard they say Bobby wet his pants and cried for mercy. Orvis never talked about this but he never really corrected the rumor either. They did have a fight, and Orvis must have won because Bobby quit bothering him and focused on other boys—me, for instance.

Orvis's final toughening moment came the night of the crab apple war.

There was a tent revival meeting that lasted the whole month of August. Aside from any religious thinking, it was pure drama for us, in the days before television, when movies at the Fox Theater only changed once a week. They put up the big tent (army surplus, of course) but kept the sides rolled down because—and I heard the minister say this—it made the women sweat and their clothes would stick to them so you could "see things." He was a small man, the minister, with a pile of hair on his head and a flashy rayon suit that changed color in the light as he moved, and he almost screamed when he preached, his voice bellowing as he ranted and tore at his collar and tie, and sometimes he spoke in gibberish and people would get up in the audience and come forward and babble in the same way and fall down and jerk around.

It was something to see. We would sneak to the back entrance to watch.

One night, after the sermon, Orvis had an idea.

We had watched it three nights running. The sermon, or the part we could understand, was always the same and the people came back each time even though they'd heard it before.

"Right toward the end," Orvis said as we walked home, "he talks about listening for the footsteps of God—tomorrow night we're going to help him."

As the tent was filling the next night, Orvis took us to the Carlsons' backyard, where they had a crab apple tree. We pulled up our T-shirts and made pouches and filled them with crab apples and went back to the tent.

Just before the minister started talking in tongues, he raised up his hands, sweat dripping down his forehead, and looked at the heavens and screamed:

"Listen! Listen for the footsteps of God!"

At that moment we threw crab apples up on the canvas tent roof and then ran around to look in the back entrance. The apples landed and rolled down the canvas, sounding for all the world like footsteps.

For half a second there was profound silence as every face turned to the roof of the tent, including the face of the minister, who looked stunned. Then men and women started screaming in tongues and falling to the ground, rolling around and jerking. I was thinking this was way better than a movie when suddenly I was jerked off my feet by a man in a suit. He had to be seven feet tall.

"Boy," he said, holding me up like a rat on a string, "what's your name and address?" Stupidly, stunned by being caught, I told him my real name and address and he came later and told my parents, and that was in the days when everybody believed in corporal punishment, so I couldn't sit down or walk right for going on a week.

The minister had a group of large, muscular men who traveled with him as organizers, to put the tent up and hang posters around town, and they were the ones who caught us.

The one who caught Orvis must have been a true monster because when he held Orvis up and asked his name Orvis became rattled and gave the first name that came to his mind. He told the man he was Archie Swenson.

This was wrong on so many different levels that it's hard to believe Orvis could have done it.

"I'm not sure why I said that," he said later. "I was maybe thinking about him, how cool he was, wondering how he would handle being caught—all in just a split second, you know—and the name just bounced out."

Archie with the good ducktail. Archie with the cigarette pack rolled in his sleeve. Archie with the engineer boots. Archie with the leather jacket.

Archie with the hot car and the half-naked girl in the steering wheel knob and the ability to flip a Zippo lighter open and set it alight for his cigarette with one snap of his fingers. Archie, rumored to have a raunchy tattoo on his chest, who might have once been in jail and who might carry a switch-blade.

That Archie.

The one name in the whole world that was certain to cause massive retribution, retaliation and a reckoning.

And once Orvis had blurted it out he couldn't pull it back, and to compound the error, as soon as he had said it he pulled free and ran off. The church man took me home, and went to find Archie the next day, whereupon he found out that Archie wasn't the one who had thrown the crab apples. The church people never did find out about Orvis.

But Archie did.

For several days Orvis lived in a kind of mute horror, waiting for the ax to fall and wondering if it might actually *be* an ax. Then he decided to act.

He waited until Archie was at work at the Texaco station and approached him. He kneeled and begged forgiveness. Archie looked down on him as royalty might look down on a subject and said, "I don't know, kid. Usually somebody does this kind of thing to me, I gotta hurt them, you know?"

"That's not a problem," Orvis said. "I'll hurt myself." And he stood up, went across the street from the gas station, turned, crouched as a runner would crouch and ran full out, as fast as his legs could pump, and slammed wide open into the brick wall next to the grease rack.

He got a concussion, was out for over ten minutes and went to the hospital in an ambulance that Archie called. Orvis became something of a legend because he left stains on the wall that lasted for years.

"The little booger almost killed himself," Archie said later in wonder. "Hell, I was just going to give him a charley horse."

But that was Orvis.

That was the same Orvis who ran into the

two things that would bring him into the Circle of Death.

Showing off.

And girls.

First, about bicycles and how they helped showing off:

There are many different kinds of bicycles now—specialty bikes, high-speed bikes, BMX bikes, stunt bikes, mountain bikes, cruisers—the list goes on and on.

Back then there were two kinds: boys' bikes, with a crossbar at the top of the frame that would cripple and emasculate you if you took a bump wrong, and girls' bikes, with a swoop-down frame that would allow a girl to ride a bike while wearing a dress without being "indecent." (It actually said that on the brochure that came with the bike, that a girl in a dress could "ride with decency.")

No boy would be caught dead riding a girls' bike and no girl would ride a boys' bike.

When a child was small he rode a tricycle and as soon as he could manage the two-wheeler he

got a full-sized bike. It was common to see children six and seven years old riding full-sized
bikes; a boy would have to stand first on one
pedal, then swing over with the off leg to reach
the other pedal, then back, because his legs
weren't long enough to reach both pedals over
the crossbar at the same time.

European bikes, with skinny tires and gears,
were all called English bikes and were looked on
with disdain as being too sissified for Americans to
ride, even though they would have been better,
faster and much more comfortable.

Americans wanted the good old-fashioned
one-speed fat-tired beasts that Schwinn and
Hawthorne made, on which you sat straight up,
and if you wanted to go faster, you simply had to
pedal harder.

Every boy who had one wanted to go faster.
And faster. And still faster.

So the first thing a boy did when he got a
bike—no matter if it was a Hawthorne Deluxe
with a chrome tank that held a battery-operated

horn and a push-button turn-signal switch and chrome fenders with a light on the front and a passenger rack and mirrors—was to strip it completely.

Off came the fenders and racks and chain guard and horn tank and mirrors and any other adornments so in the end you pretty much had two wheels and a sprocket attached to a frame.

Stripping down brought on a change in the boys as well. It's not that we became outlaws (although there were some who thought of us that way) so much as we just wanted to really, really push the envelope. In those days, people just said, "Look, there go those crazy boys again, trying to kill themselves."

And to be honest it would sometimes appear that way.

The thing is that without television we had very few role models, and the ones that got the most press were not always true sports figures.

Instead, we read about daredevils.

These were men who jumped cars and motor-cycles over ramps through hoops of fire, rolled cars, crashed cars, lit *themselves* on fire, climbed into boxes filled with dynamite and set it off, had themselves shot out of cannons and did any num-ber of wonderful and wild things that we all, to a boy, were pretty sure we could emulate if we just got our Schwinns going fast enough or high enough or hard enough.

Every year at the county fair they would come crashing and banging and burning and rolling, all to the screams of crowds and the roar of unmuffled engines.

And many of them had their own daredevil shows. Hardly a month went by in the summer and fall without somebody setting up at the fairgrounds or in a field, anywhere they could get up a crowd, with old cars or motorcycles and ramps.

We all loved it and between shows would try the stunts on our own.

We built countless ramps with old boards laid on barrels or boxes, at the bottom of a hill if possible, and we would try to jump over things with our bikes.

Remember, these were one-speed fat-tired bikes with a crowned-up, castrating brace bar and the things we tried to jump were fences, wooden walls, barrels, bikes, each other. On one memorable occasion Alan—after carefully calculating distances and angles—tried to jump his stepfather's Ford coupe end to end. He didn't ... quite ... make it and left a face print on the windshield of the car, but that might have been because he was distracted by the scream when his mother came out just as we finished the ramp and Alan made his jump.

These are images I will carry to my grave:

Orvis zooming down Black Hill, where a road went almost straight down the riverbank in a near-vertical drop, and missing the ramp board with his front tire, slamming into the old wooden barrels we'd put up for a jump obstacle, cartwheeling with his bicycle past the barrels, skipping twice in the dirt and bouncing clean, still hanging on to his bicycle, out over the riverbank and into the water. It was shallow there, and he stood up, covered in mud and weeds, and held up his hand and yelled, "I declined the jump! I declined the jump!" He had seen riders jumping horses on the newsreel and said that if you declined the jump it was legal to miss.

Alan, again after carefully calculating and measuring (I never quite figured out where he got all the figures and thought it might have something to do with him being smarter because of the Canadian blood), decided that if you got up to twenty-six miles an hour and angled a ramp to ensure (that's how he put it, "to ensure") that you got at least seven point six feet in the air, it was possible to do a complete backward somersault and land on your wheels upright. Alan, having gotten at least seven feet in the air after a screaming run down Black Hill, landed exactly, perfectly upside down, bicycle wheels straight up, spinning, in a cloud of dust and gravel. And then, after carefully calculating and measuring, and not a little bandaging, Alan raised his hand and said, "Aha, my calculations were for a forward somersault, not a backward flip," as if it really mattered. Then Alan again, leaving the ground like a rocket up the ramp, easily eight feet in the air this time, and landing upside down again.

Alan tried once more, getting a lift from an unsuspecting truck by hanging on to the rear corner and hitting the ramp so fast that it gave way and he went through it like a tank, barrels and boards and splinters flying everywhere.

Wayne completed the only true backward flip off a bicycle but he didn't take the bike with him.

We had become more and more proficient at crashing and bashing, as we called stunting, just like the posters that advertised the daredevil shows. We'd even decided that if we got just a little better we might put on a proper show and charge admission and thereby make A Lot of Money.

Wayne wanted to perfect his favorite trick, which was to jump a line of three barrels and at the top let go of the handlebars, turn sideways and wave and smile, just like a man named Rock-eting Red, who jumped a motorcycle over two cars, turned and waved, landed and rode through a Hoop of Flame! We had talked Wayne out of the hoop of flame with some difficulty—pointing out that if we lit up a hoop of flame anywhere in town we would all probably wind up in jail, if we were lucky—but he had a good smile and was proud of it. So one afternoon we all set up the ramp and barrels and Wayne got ready for his practice run.

As it turned out we didn't have time to get all the stuff to the bottom of Black Hill and so we just set it up near the Seversons' backyard, which was where we usually set it up for short runs, but there was a major difference now.

Its name was King.

The Seversons were a sweet elderly couple without a mean bone in their bodies but their son Curt had gone off to the army and had left his dog with his parents.

King was perhaps a third pit bull, a third Doberman and about a third crocodile—the meanest animal on four legs. The Seversons kept him tied on a chain in their backyard, where he had watched us whipping by on our bicycles on many days, roaring and slavering to get at us, tearing at the earth, ripping up clods of sod and dirt, grinding his bared teeth and hating us, hating bicycles, hating air, hating the world.

And this morning Wayne came careening down the alley, took the jump, turned sideways and smiled and waved at an imaginary crowd just as King made a lunge and found to his everlasting joy that his chain had broken free from his collar.

You've got to hand it to Wayne. He knew instantly that he was in trouble. He hit the ground still smiling—or it might have become a grimace of horror—and stood on the pedals, looking for speed.

He had been moving pretty well to make the jump and had a fair lead. I saw gravel spurt from his rear tire as he slammed the pedals down and I thought he might just outrun King, and in fact I was thinking that if he *did* outrun King there was a good chance the beast would be coming back after us, and I was wondering about taking off in the other direction to get up my own head of speed when Wayne made his mistake.

Instead of barreling straight down the alley, he thought—as he told us a week later, when he could speak again—that if he cut through the Nelsons' backyard and got out in the street it might confuse the dog.

So he angled right, really moving now, just a blur, with King coming after him—and ran into the Nelsons' clothesline.

Mr. Nelson had worked hard on that clothesline. He had set four-inch steel posts in concrete and strung four quarter-inch-thick steel cables to hang the clothes on, and Wayne caught not the first but the last cable under his chin and it took him off that bike as if a giant hand had come down from the sky and plucked him away.

Up, up, his feet went in a beautiful arc.

Both feet straight out, the bike traveling on, Wayne's body swinging up and up and back over the top of the line and then down to land across all four clothesline cables and then bounce onto the ground.

King was there in an instant. I thought, Lord, the dog will kill him.

But the dog went past him and attacked the bicycle. It was bicycles he hated and he tore both tires off while Wayne sat up and pointed at his throat, which had a red line across it, and then fell over to the side sucking air and making a sound like a broken vacuum cleaner.

A perfect backward somersault off a bicycle.

4

Girls, and the Circle of Death

Girls.

When we were eleven and even twelve they were just like us.

Sort of.

That is, we could be friends and do projects together in school and some boys could even talk to them.

Not me. I never could. And neither could Orvis. Alan seemed to have worked out a way to pretend they weren't even there and Wayne, who had had that experience with the power supply for the picture tube on the back of the television set, swore that it didn't bother him at all to speak to girls.

And then we became thirteen.

Everything changed.

Well, not everything. I still couldn't talk to them, lived in mortal terror of them, and Orvis was the same way. But we talked *about* them all the time, how they looked, how they smiled, how they sounded, how they must think, about life, about us, how Elaine was really cute but Eileen had prettier hair and Eileen seemed one day to actually, actually look at me, right at me. But we couldn't speak *to* them.

Except that now it became very important that we be *able* to speak to them. Before, it didn't seem to matter, and now it was somehow the only thing that *did* matter. I even approached Wayne one day and asked him what he thought about me coming over and touching the back of his television set but he pointed out that (a) it was just luck that it hadn't killed him and (b) it had had some bad side effects for a couple of weeks involving bed-wetting and strange dreams about a robot made of electricity and chewing gum that I probably didn't want to deal with.

Still, I had this problem because Eileen actually *had* looked at me one day on the way out of school, or so I thought, and on top of it she had smiled—I was pretty sure at me as well—and I thought that maybe I was In Love and that it was For Real and when I asked Orvis about it he agreed that I might be In Love for Real and suggested that I take Eileen to a movie.

Which nearly stopped my heart cold. I couldn't talk to her—how could I ask her to go to a movie? Finally it was Orvis who thought of the way. I would ask Wayne to ask Shirley Johnson to ask Claudia Erskine, who was a close friend of Eileen's, if Eileen might like to go to the movies with me the following Saturday afternoon.

This tortuous procedure was actually followed and by the time I was told that indeed Eileen would like to see a movie the next Saturday, I was a nervous wreck and honestly hoped she wouldn't go.

We met in front of the theater, as things were done then at our age—I couldn't even imagine going to her home and ringing the bell to pick her up and having her parents answer the door. If I couldn't really speak to girls, what in god's name would I do with a set of *parents* of the girl I was going to take to a movie?

So we met at the theater at one-thirty. I wore what I thought were my best clothes, a pullover sweater over a turtleneck, with my feeble attempt at a flattop, Butch-Waxed so much that dropping an anvil on my head wouldn't have flattened it. I think now I must have looked something like a really uncomfortable, sweaty, walking, greasy-topped bottle brush. (Have I mentioned that with my sweater and turtleneck I had gone solely for fashion and had ignored the fact that it was high summer? Or that the theater was most decidedly *not* air-conditioned?)

But Eileen was a nice person and pretended not to notice the sweat filling my shoes so they sloshed when we walked or how I dropped my handful of money all over the ground. I had brought all of my seven dollars in savings because I really didn't know how much it would cost, what with tickets and treats, and maybe she was a big eater.

She also pretended not to notice when I asked her if she wanted popcorn.

So I asked her again. Louder.

And then again. Louder.

All because I was blushing so hard my ears were ringing and I wasn't sure if I was really making a sound and so when I screamed it out the third time and she jumped back, it more or less set the tone for the whole date.

We went into the theater all right. And we sat next to each other. And she was kind enough to overlook the fact that I smelled like a dead buffalo and that other than asking her three times if she wanted popcorn I didn't say a word to her. Not a word.

I couldn't.

The movie was called *The Thing,* about a creature from another planet who crashes to earth in the Arctic and develops a need/thirst/obsession for human and sled-dog blood and isn't killed until they figure out that he's really a kind of walking, roaring, grunting plant. So they rig up some wire to "cook him like a stewed carrot." All of this I learned the second time around, when I went to the movie with Wayne, because sitting next to Eileen, pouring sweat, giving her endless boxes of Dots and candy corn and popcorn (almost none of which she wanted but accepted nicely and set on the seat next to her), I didn't remember a single thing about the movie. Not a word, not a scene.

All I could do was sit and think, I'm this close to a girl, right next to a girl, my arm almost touching her arm, a girl, right there, right *there*. . . .

It was a nightmare. The movie seemed to last two, three weeks; I know I aged at least ten years. When at last it was over and she headed home (I should have walked her there but I didn't dare), all I could think of was the relief. I had done it. I had gone on a date. Though we would never do it again—I would never ask her and I'm certain if I had she would not have gone—I had done it. And I had spoken to her.

"WOULD YOU LIKE SOME POPCORN?"

A scream, to be sure, but I had taken a girl to a movie and sat next to her the whole time and I think my arm may have touched her arm somewhere along the way, or at least it felt that way through the sweater and turtleneck and I had finally done it. An extra benefit was that I had also learned just why those things are called sweaters.

But the reason I bring up this whole disaster of my first date, and my fear of girls, is to show that as terrified and shy as I was, as horrified of being with a girl, talking to a girl, as awful as I turned out to be...

Orvis was worse.

He was clinically shy, could hardly even look at girls, and wanted desperately to be able to do so.

So he evolved a method for getting attention from girls: showing off.

Suddenly it wasn't good enough just to make the bikes jump a ramp or do a stunt; he had to do it in front of girls. And it wasn't enough just to do a stunt in front of girls; he had to do it higher and farther and harder.

And in a more dangerous way.

Here is where Orvis came into his own. Somehow he mixed the ability to do stunts of truly amazing risk with the absolute fearlessness he had demonstrated when he ran into the wall of the gas station where Archie worked. He didn't seem to care if he was injured. As long as a girl was watching he would try anything.

We would jump over two barrels, so he would try to clear three; we would try to get eight feet in the air, he would try for ten. We would try landing with no feet on the pedals, he would land with no hands on the handlebars *or* feet on the pedals.

He crashed and bashed and flopped and flipped and cartwheeled and somersaulted until even when he was standing still he seemed to be a blur and all we had to do was say, "Look, there's Margaret," or "Elaine" or "Judy," and he was tearing off on his bike, bouncing off a curb and flying through the air.

Finally, this led Orvis to the Circle of Death.

■ ■ ■

County fairs now are fun and there are wild rides to go on and bad candy and antique hot dogs and clip joints to take your money for throwing a ball or pitching a coin onto a plate or tossing a ring over an impossible peg. All of that was the same back then, except there were other things that aren't allowed anymore:

Sideshows with strange people and animals and closed tents where there were large glass jars full of alcohol and some really *ugly* body parts. Wild things. Snakes with two heads or human kidneys in the shape of Rhode Island. There was usually a strip show, called the "Hootchy Cootchy Dancers," where women well past forty would dance to raspy music and take their clothes off. We never got into those tents because we were too young and even if you went around to the back and tried to peek under the canvas they had a second flap hanging down inside that made it impossible to see anything, and even if you somehow got past the second flap all you saw was the back of the stage. Or so I'm told.

And there would be the "Wild Man from Borneo!" show that had a half-naked man in a pit, wearing rags, who would pretend to be the missing link trapped in the jungles and bite the heads off live chickens.

Ah, those were the good old days, before there was all this control. If it sounds a bit weird, the history of fairs in medieval times is even more bizarre; for a couple of centuries there was a contest, a wildly popular sporting event that involved hanging a live cat from a post and killing it by beating it to death with your *face*. It was taken very seriously and men who were good at it became grand heroes. Talk about extreme sports—you have to wonder what tailgate parties would have been like. This makes even golf look sane.

But back to *our* fairs. Along with the rides and body parts in alcohol and strippers and other good times there was the Circle of Death.

Or Pit of Death.

Or bear pit.

It was a small boxing ring set up in the center of the midway. A man with a trained bear would stand in the middle of the ring on the canvas and keep the bear on a leash—the bear was also wearing a muzzle—and people could pay a quarter to get into the ring and test their strength by "wrestling" the bear. A big sign read:

STAY IN THE RING WITH BRUNO FOR ONE MINUTE AND WIN TWENTY-FIVE DOLLARS!

Of course it sounds silly. Bears are immensely strong. No human on earth could wrestle one and win. It just couldn't be done.

And yet . . .

The bear pit was as popular as beating a cat to death with your face was in the Dark Ages. (And probably for similar psychological reasons.) Young men from the farms were always looking for ways to prove their strength and they flocked to the Circle of Death and we flocked there to watch them pay their quarters and get thrown out of the ring.

And what's more, Bruno seemed to like it. He would stand in the middle of the ring on his back legs, weaving slightly, his trainer next to him, watching as the next victim climbed in. The bear actually knew how to wrestle. He probably weighed four hundred pounds and could easily have flattened an opponent with a swing of his paw. But he didn't hit. Instead he would get into the stance, one paw on his opponent's shoulder, the other on his arm, and they would lean into each other and the handler would yell, "Go!" and Bruno would simply throw the other man out of the ring.

Then he would get a bottle of Coca-Cola, which his trainer would open and hold up to his mouth. Bruno would drain it and emit a huge belch before getting ready for the next farm boy.

Of course we were too cool to try wrestling the bear. Or too chicken. It amounts to the same thing. We would watch and cheer the bear and tease the farm workers—although not excessively, considering how strong they looked—but we didn't really think of climbing into the Circle of Death.

One day we were watching the bear wrestle, and laughing, and when I happened to glance at Orvis I saw a strange look come into his eye. It was very similar to the look Carl had after viewing the newsreel about breaking the speed record on skis.

"Are you all right?"

He nodded. "I'm fine, why?"

"You looked at the bear kind of funny...."

"Not the bear so much as the sign. Did you see that sign?"

"What about it?"

"It doesn't say anything about actually beating the bear at wrestling. It just says you have to stay in the ring with him for one minute."

"Orvis..."

"I think if you just hung on to the bear—"

"Orvis, that's a bear. A real bear. One minute is

a long time. There's farm boys here who could pinch your head like a pimple and they can't stay in there with Bruno."

"Loan me a quarter. I'll pay you back when I get the twenty-five dollars."

All right, I know what you're thinking; that twenty-five cents was a lot of money to waste, that Orvis wouldn't make a good bicep on those farm boys, let alone be a problem for a bear. But, remember, I still had that scientific curiosity and I was starting to wonder just what *would* happen if Orvis took a try at the bear.

So I gave him a quarter.

And he stepped into the ring and took the stance with the bear.

Orvis came out of the ring a little faster than he went in—of course the bear tossed him out— but he got up and dusted his pants off. I said a permanent goodbye to my quarter and had started to walk away when I heard soft giggling and looked up to see Elaine, Eileen and Margaret watching Orvis and laughing. I thought, Oh no, and turned to pull him away. Too late. Orvis had seen the girls.

"Give me another quarter."

"Orvis . . ."

"Now."

"I don't think it's a good idea."

"*Now!*"

It was as if I weren't there. It was just Orvis and the girls.

And, oh yeah, the bear. Let's not forget the bear.

I talked to the trainer later while we were bandaging Orvis. The trainer was a nice guy, and so was the bear, who really did love to wrestle. "But he has his pride, too," the trainer told me. "Bruno has his pride." The thing is, the bear had trained himself after countless contests to match the strength of his opponent; he would kindly feel the other person out, then just apply enough extra strength to win the match.

But he hated it if they came back a second time. "It's like they don't believe him," the trainer said. "Like he was being nice and they didn't believe it, so when they come back he makes it a little worse for them."

That would begin to describe what happened to Orvis: The bear made it worse for him.

I still do not believe you can do those things to a human body without breaking it.

Orvis took the stance, the bear took the stance, the handler pocketed his quarter and looked at Orvis and asked, "Are you ready?"

Orvis nodded, the trainer said, "Go!" and the fight was on.

Well, it wasn't a fight so much as Orvis just trying to stay alive. Initially the bear decided to make it just a little worse, and with one paw on Orvis's shoulder he used the other paw at Orvis's stomach to bend him in the middle, pound his butt down to the ground, fold him over like he was folding a piece of paper and slam Orvis's face down between his own knees on the canvas so hard I saw snot fly out of Orvis's nose. Whereupon the bear held him flat that way and calmly used his other paw to scoot Orvis out of the ring under the bottom rope. Kind of like a big hockey puck with legs.

Except that Orvis didn't go.

As the bear tried to push him out Orvis grabbed a back leg and held on. ("I looked up and through the haze I saw the girls watching," he told me later.) This new tactic surprised the bear and he danced back into the center of the ring.

Dragging Orvis back with him. Which could be a good thing, as Orvis thought much, much later. Or a very, very bad thing, as Orvis thought at the moment.

He was still in the ring and I heard somebody say, "The kid's made twenty seconds."

For a beat—actually it was three seconds; I had started counting, thinking I might somehow get my quarters back—the bear looked down, as if studying him, at Orvis hanging on to his back leg.

Then the bear bent down and, using both paws, picked Orvis up, fashioned him into something like a ball and shot-putted him out of the ring.

Or tried to.

Just as Orvis was leaving the bear's paws his

hand reached back and grabbed a chunk of fur on the bear's shoulder and hung on. Orvis swung up and over in a tight arc and landed on top of the bear's head.

Big mistake, I thought.

"Thirty-five seconds," the same man yelled, and then they all began chanting, "Thirty-six, thirty-seven, thirty-eight..." And I looked over and saw that the girls weren't giggling any longer, and they were counting too. "... Thirty-nine, forty..."

For the bear, having Orvis land on his head was the last straw, and what followed were the longest twenty seconds in Orvis's life.

The bear bundled Orvis into a ball and virtually dribbled him around the ring, batting him back and forth, flipping him in the air like a toy, catching him, dropping him to the ground and flipping him up again, at one point sitting on him while he braided Orvis's legs together. Orvis wouldn't admit it later but I swore that, girls or no girls, at one point he tried to crawl out of the ring.

But the bear dragged him back and kept working on him until finally the trainer, pulling on the leash, got him off Orvis and the man next to me yelled, "He made it! Give the kid twenty-five dollars!" and we were all cheering and the girls were jumping up and down and waving and even Bruno looked happy as the trainer gave him a Coke.

The trainer and I pulled Orvis onto a stool in the corner and wiped the dust out of his eyes and the trainer gave him a towel to use to clean himself up a little. Orvis looked as if he'd been pulled through a knothole backward. Then the trainer got out some bandages and we started covering the scrapes and minor cuts from hitting various things around the ring, like the floor, and the corner posts, and the floor, and again the floor. Then the trainer gave Orvis two tens and a five and right then the girls came up to him.

"That was great—you were great!" they said, surrounding him, and they smiled and laughed and they were laughing with and not at him but it didn't matter. He didn't say a word, couldn't say a word, and they walked off shaking their heads and Bruno, I swear, put out a paw and gently ruffled the hair on Orvis's head.

"Nice girls," the trainer said, but Orvis was just staring down at the floor, his head wobbling only a little as he tried to focus on his feet. Then he looked up at me and in a plaintive little puppy dog voice he asked:

"Wasn't I wearing shoes when we came?"

5

And Finally, Skateboards, Bungee Jumping and Other Failures

We had to make our own skateboards.

I know that sounds ridiculous but there was no such thing then.

We took a three-foot-long piece of two-by-six board, hopefully with no knot in the middle because—as Wayne found out when he tried a small jump at near-terminal velocity—the board will break where the knot is if you come down on it hard. We nailed skate wheels at each end with roofing nails. Roller skates were these god-awful four-wheeled metal monster things that clamped to your shoes with a wrench called a skate key—a lot of fun if you were wearing tennis shoes, or, as we called them then, PF Flyers, the brand name. There were wonderful cartoon ads in comic books and *Boys' Life* magazine about how a boy could run fast and do heroic things, like warn people of a flood or run to save a train by telling the engineer the bridge was out, and all because he was wearing PF Flyers.

The skates had miserable bearings that filled with sand very fast and the only good thing about them was that they came apart easily and had little holes where you could drive the roofing nails into the wood.

And so, a skateboard.

At first we tried to nail a box to one end and make a kind of scooter, but that almost always blew up in our faces when we'd hit a bump and wind up wearing the box over our heads.

Now, it's one thing to have a skateboard—it's something else to have a place to use it. This is obviously still a problem, judging by the numbers of boys destroying their groins on handrails. Back then there was no such thing as a skateboard park, there were no malls with large parking lots, and sidewalks were full of people and were badly cracked and broken from frost heaves anyway. That left just one place.

The streets.

We spent most of our time in the summer skateboarding in traffic, or hopefully in and *out* of traffic, and that led to what we called hitching.

There we were on the boards, and cars were going by, and it was just a matter of time before one of us grabbed on to one of the car bumpers and hitched a ride.

We thought we were being clever but it's difficult to describe just how stupid this was; the cars weighed about a ton, we weighed about a hundred pounds, the cars were made of steel, we were made of flesh—or, as Alan said, dumb meat—the cars couldn't feel pain, we could, the cars could go fast....

And we wanted to go fast. We would grab bumpers and crouch down so the drivers couldn't see us, because there were no outside mirrors then on cars, and most trunks humped up and blocked any view of the back end of the car from the rearview mirror inside. We'd ride a block, then two—sometimes four or five blocks across our small town.

And if one guy went two blocks, naturally somebody else had to do three, or five, or seven. . . .

Which is how Wayne came to establish the distance record for skateboarding.

Well, there came a Saturday morning in August when the sun was hot and the sky was clear and blue and Orvis pulled a classic double right in front of us. We were standing on a corner, our scabby boards hanging at our sides, when Orvis jumped out, caught a Hudson (a favorite car because it had a huge humped trunk and tiny rear window), hitched half a block while we watched, let go of the Hudson and, still coasting in a crouch, caught a '51 Buick coming back toward us and wheeled to a standing stop right in front of us—an absolutely perfect double hitch.

"Big deal," Wayne said. He was still smarting over the fact that Orvis had won twenty-five dollars with the bear, and Wayne needed money because he wanted to buy a new bow before bow-hunting deer season. "Watch this."

And he picked a car going by, crouched down, and grabbed on. We watched him leave, heading into the distance. We were on the edge of town and in moments he was out of sight, moving down the highway and around a curve into the country.

We waited, and waited, and finally we hitched back into town and went to the drugstore to have Coke glasses filled with ice cream covered with chocolate sauce and peanuts which were called, I swear, Little Dicks. There was a sign that we could not look at without smiling that read:

LITTLE DICKS
15 CENTS

Then we hitched back out to the edge of town by Black Hill. They had recently asphalted the hill road for about an eighth of a mile and we were learning to kind of lie back on our boards and race each other down the hill. It was a crude attempt at what would later be called luge racing and would have been a lot of fun except that at the bottom of the hill the road was coarse gravel and at high speed it was like running into a giant electric belt sander.

We had been there an hour or so and were comparing road rashes when Wayne appeared at the top of the hill and whipped down into the gravel next to us.

"I went to Hutchinson," he said, "and back."

Hutchinson was a town seven miles away. He had only been gone two hours or so.

"There's no way," Alan said, "that you could have hitched the distance to Hutchinson and back in two hours."

"Yeah, really. I took the car you saw me with all the way over and hung around and had a Coke and then caught a chicken truck back. Here, smell my arm."

He *did* smell like chicken manure, but even so, fourteen miles down a highway on a skateboard . . .

I figured he hitchhiked back and caught a ride on a chicken truck. Orvis thought he just went a little way out of town and then hitchhiked back.

But somebody on the sidewalk in Hutchinson had taken a picture of him catching the back end of the chicken truck. In the background is a perfectly clear picture of Hutchinson Hardware.

And because Wayne has the worst luck in the world and fame always has a price, the picture appeared on the front page of the Hutchinson *Clarion* under the headline:

WILD KIDS CATCH WILD RIDES

Wayne's father saw the paper and took Wayne and his skateboard out into the garage and broke the skateboard. Wayne swore it was over his head but there wasn't a mark there, while he had trouble sitting down for nearly a week.

But he still has the record. Fourteen miles.

■ ■ ■

To understand what might have been the first bungee jump you have to understand my cousin Harris.

I wrote about him in *Harris and Me*—how he discovered rodeo, and Tarzan, and tried to make a motorcycle with a bicycle and a gasoline-powered washing machine motor, which almost worked until he accidentally tried to clear two acres of brush at the end of the driveway with his body.

The thing is, Harris believed, completely, in himself. Whether it was fighting the pet lynx or diving into the pigpen, which he pretended was a fort full of "commie bastards," he felt he was absolutely unable to fail.

Even when he did fail, he thought he was successful.

The bungee jumping came about because Harris's father had to change the tires on their only tractor.

The tubes in the back tires were shot and his father pulled them out and replaced them. While the tires wouldn't hold air, they could still be used for other things.

Inner tubes then were made of pure rubber and were wonderfully elastic. You could carefully cut strips out of a car inner tube about an inch wide and a foot and a half long and make a great slingshot that would zing a round rock fast enough to break a bottle at twenty-five yards or put a heck of a welt on Wayne's butt if he had just shot *you* in the butt with a small rock.

But something as big as tractor inner tubes, with their thicker rubber and large size, fairly screamed for some greater use.

"We could make a really *big* slingshot," Harris said. "Tie it between two trees and shoot ourselves across the yard. Maybe into the sky."

"No," I said, shaking my head, "we'd have to come down."

"Hmmm." He thought a moment and then smiled. "That's it."

"What is?"

"Coming down. We can tie a rope to the inner

tube and then another rope under our armpits and we'll get a good bounce out of it. It'll be just like them parachute soldiers when they jumped on the commie bastards." Harris's concept of history was a little blurred. He knew there had been a Second World War but the country right then was in the middle of the communist scare and he mixed the two up.

I was ten and he was eight, and I already had my healthy curiosity. "How will you get a good bounce out of that?"

"Simple, you gooner. We'll tie it to the top of the barn roof and jump out the hayloft door."

And it was about that easy to set it up. There was a pulley at the peak of the barn for pulling hay up inside off hayracks, and Harris tied the rope to the pulley, then tied the other end to the inner tubes. He used both of them, side by side, and pulled the long part of the rope up to the peak of the roof, just outside the loft door.

The inner tubes were even with his head, where he stood up in the big barn door opening, and he took another piece of old rope, made two loops through the inner tubes and tucked it up into his armpits, yelled something unrepeatable and, with complete confidence, jumped out the hayloft door.

The bounce part worked. I was standing slightly to the side to watch and I can vouch for that, although the rope was just a bit too long.

He went down like a shot, both inner tubes stretching nicely, and just as his face slapped the dirt they retracted and snapped him back up into the air.

Except he didn't come straight back up. He had gone down at a slight angle and there was a low eave over the milk room at that end of the barn that stuck out about two feet.

Harris came up under the eave and smashed into a wasps' nest.

The wasps had absolutely no tolerance for bungee jumping and they swarmed on him as he headed back down for the ground, hit once more, then snapped back up and cleared the milk room eave, out into the open air, trailed by a swarm of wasps that had decided to use him for target practice.

"Cut the rope! Cut the rope!" he screamed, but I had no knife and had to untie the end he had tied to the barn and my ability to untie the rope was greatly handicapped by the fact that I was laughing hysterically.

"Cut the damn rope!"

Finally I got it loose and he landed on the ground in a buzzing, screaming heap and started running for the stock tank to jump in the water but he was still affixed to the inner tubes and the rope became entangled, so just as he got up a good head of steam, about eight feet short of the stock tank the rope caught, stretched the tubes and yanked him back a good ten feet, flat on his butt, where the wasps got him again.

"Them parachute soldiers really got guts," he said later, as we were dabbing mud on his swollen, wasp-stung face. "I wouldn't do that again even *without* the wasps."

■ ■ ■

Along with all the extreme sports I've described, there were attempts at stunts and sports that never quite jelled.

Wayne decided to crawl into a box with dynamite and set it off like the daredevils at the fair except that we didn't have any dynamite (a really good thing) so he crawled into an old refrigerator carton and we used three full-force M-80 firecrackers with the fuses wrapped to go off at the same time. The box didn't blow up at all, and the only result was that for two weeks every time you asked Wayne a question he would say, *"What? What?"* and he kept slapping at mosquitoes buzzing around his head when there weren't any mosquitoes.

Orvis decided to take a try at the hoop of fire and against our advice made a wooden frame covered with burlap ("Just like they do at the fair," he said), which he soaked in kerosene. We stood by with buckets of water as Wayne lit the frame and Orvis backed off and got a good run at it before jumping his bike from the ramp through the center of the fire. It looked spectacular, with flames and smoke flying after him, and it could have been worse—his hair was slow to come back, but he had a pretty good crop of fuzz inside a month. The sad thing was that he actually got through the hoop when there were no girls around and Alan, who was standing by with the Brownie camera, forgot to take the picture.

Then there was Angel of the skis again with an army surplus full-sized parachute and his attempt to use it as a sail with ice skates on Lake Oosshta, which worked fine until a gust of wind pulled him off his feet and the chute rope that was knotted around his stomach slipped down to catch one leg and he was pulled some four miles across the lake, backward on his stomach. And then during the summer Angel tried to use the parachute as a sail on his bicycle, only to have a gust flip him over and drag him and his bike a quarter mile down a gravel road. Then there was Angel's

attempt to use the parachute as a sail on a bor-
rowed canoe, only to have a gust flip him over
and tangle him in the shroud lines and almost
drown him. Then, at last, there was Angel selling
the chute to the neighbors, who used it for a yard
awning.

And then finally, Wayne again, who read a
book that said the hero had made a diving bell by
using a bucket over his head and some kind of
hose arrangement to keep air coming from a tire
pump. Even with Orvis pumping as hard as he
could, Wayne nearly drowned under the Fourth
Street Bridge on the Mud River, where he swears
to this day that he felt a shark brush past him
in the dark water. He always says that: "It
brushed past me in the dark water." There are of
course no freshwater sharks in the Mud River in
northern Minnesota—although the water is dark
enough, being mostly mud—but you can't tell
Wayne that, just as you couldn't tell Orvis he
couldn't beat the bear or Angel he couldn't beat
the speed record on skis or Emil he couldn't fly
the target kite because, like Harris, we also

believed in ourselves and what we could do or thought we could do. It didn't matter that it hadn't been done before. It was still worth trying.

It was, always, worth the try.

GARY PAULSEN is the distinguished author of many critically acclaimed books for young people, including three Newbery Honor books: *The Winter Room, Hatchet* and *Dogsong*. His novel *The Haymeadow* received the Western Writers of America Golden Spur Award. Among his newest Random House books are *Caught by the Sea: My Life on Boats, Guts: The True Stories Behind* Hatchet *and the Brian Books, The Beet Fields: Memories of a Sixteenth Summer, Alida's Song* (a companion to *The Cookcamp*), *Soldier's Heart, The Transall Saga, My Life in Dog Years, Sarny: A Life Remembered* (a companion to *Nightjohn*), *Brian's Return* and *Brian's Winter* (companions to *Hatchet*), *Father Water, Mother Woods: Essays on Fishing and Hunting in the North Woods* and five books about Francis Tucket's adventures in the Old West. Gary Paulsen has also published fiction and nonfiction for adults, as well as picture books illustrated by his wife, the painter Ruth Wright Paulsen. Their most recent book is *Canoe Days*. The Paulsens live in New Mexico and on the Pacific Ocean.